P9-DIF-821

Dear Parent:

Your child's love of reading starts here!

Every child learns to read in a different way and at his or her own speed. Some go back and forth between reading levels and read favorite books again and again. Others read through each level in order. You can help your young reader improve and become more confident by encouraging his or her own interests and abilities. From books your child reads with you to the first books he or she reads alone, there are I Can Read Books for every stage of reading:

SHARED READING
Basic language, word repetition, and whimsical illustrations, ideal for sharing with your emergent reader

BEGINNING READING
Short sentences, familiar words, and simple concepts for children eager to read on their own

READING WITH HELP
Engaging stories, longer sentences, and language play for developing readers

READING ALONE
Complex plots, challenging vocabulary, and high-interest topics for the independent reader

I Can Read Books have introduced children to the joy of reading since 1957. Featuring award-winning authors and illustrators and a fabulous cast of beloved characters, I Can Read Books set the standard for beginning readers.

A lifetime of discovery begins with the magical words **"I Can Read!"**

Visit www.icanread.com for information on enriching your child's reading experience.

Library of Congress Control Number: 2019956229
ISBN 978-0-06-265480-9 (trade bdg.) — ISBN 978-0-06-265479-3 (pbk.)

Book design by Chrisila Maida

20 21 22 23 24 LSCC 10 9 8 7 6 5 4 3 2 1 ❖ First Edition

Mike Berenstain

Based on the characters created by
Stan and Jan Berenstain

HARPER
An Imprint of HarperCollins*Publishers*

Bear Country School is having

a talent show.

Any student can be in the show.

All you need is a talent.

Teacher Jane is in charge.

She will choose acts for the show.

The cubs show off their talents.

Teacher Jane checks them off.

First, there's a magic act.

Check!

Then, there's a rap group.

Check!

One cub does a tap dance.

Another wiggles his ears.

Cousin Fred rubs his tummy
and pats his head.
It isn't much of a talent.
But he's very good at it!

Now it's Brother's and Sister's turn.

Brother plays the drums.

He plays very loud!

Sister sings.

She sings loud, too!

Barry is up next.

Barry's dog does tricks.

His dog sits up.

His dog lies down.

Barry's dog rolls over.

He stands on his hind legs.

Then he does a dance.

He does a hula dance.

It’s a good act!

Now Suzy goes onstage.

She opens her mouth.

She opens it very wide.

Then Suzy starts to yodel.

Suzy is a good yodeler.

She yodels high.

She yodels low.

She yodels all over the place!

All the cubs clap.

"My goodness, Suzy!" says Teacher Jane.

"You surely can yodel!"

Suzy blushes.

"My uncle Otto taught me," she says.

More cubs go onstage.

They have all sorts of talents.

“We have talents, enough, now,” says

Teacher Jane.

“Our talent show is ready.”

The show is on the very next day.

The big school talent show is about to begin.
The cubs in the show peek out from the stage.

There's a very big crowd!

The curtain goes up.

One after another, the cubs go on.

They have lots of talent!

Near the end, Barry's dog
does his tricks.

Last of all, Suzy yodels.

She yodels up a storm!

Everyone claps and cheers.

It's time to choose the best talent.
Teacher Jane holds a hand over
each cub.
Everyone claps.

But they clap the loudest for Suzy.

Everyone likes yodeling.

All the talented cubs take a bow.

The school talent show is a big hit!